All the King's Animals

All the King's Animals
The Return of Endangered Wildlife to Swaziland

Written and photographed by Cristina Kessler
With a foreword by Mswati III, King of Swaziland

Boyds Mills Press

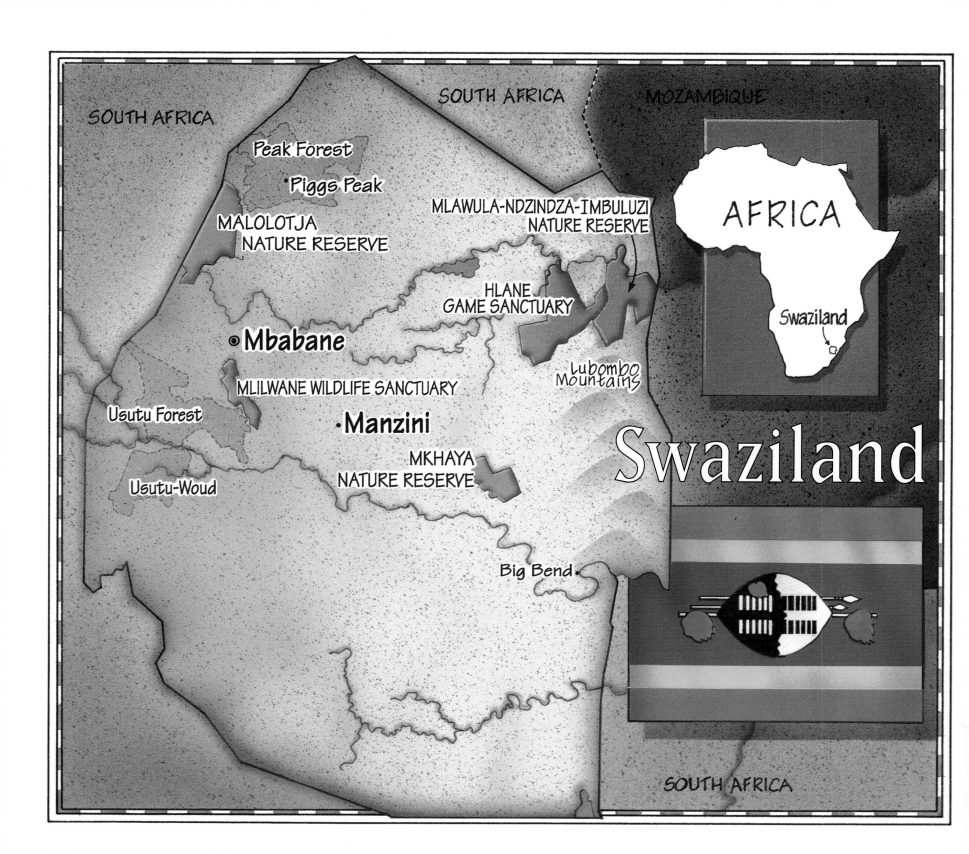

Contents

STATE HOUSE
KINGDOM OF SWAZILAND

FOREWORD BY HIS MAJESTY, KING MSWATI III, INGWENYAMA OF THE KINGDOM OF SWAZILAND

Some of my earliest memories of childhood are of days spent with my father, the legendary King Sobhuza II, in our country's lowveld, enjoying the sights and sounds of Swaziland's wildlife and learning of the relationship between our people and the land that God gave us. On one such occasion, we were sitting within the grounds of a royal residence when a commotion of noise and activity from His Majesty's bodyguards drew our attention away from our discussion. A snake had suddenly appeared quite close to the royal group, and the king's men rushed to attack it with knives drawn and knobkerries held high. But King Sobhuza called them back. "Why are you so intent on destroying one of God's creatures?" he asked. "This place is the snake's home. He was here long before us. We are intruders on his territory. We must learn to live together in harmony with all who share our world." The snake was allowed to slither to freedom, and a young prince never forgot the wise words of his father.

The animals, the birds, the rivers, and the forests were indeed here long before us. It is mankind's duty to protect them, and it is a duty that Swaziland very nearly failed to uphold. This book tells the story of how my country, under the guidance of King Sobhuza II and the devotion of one man, Ted "Machobane" Reilly, managed to fulfill its duty to the rest of the world by bringing back the animals we had once lost. As a child, I was lucky to sit at the feet of a man who believed passionately in the conservation of the natural order of his kingdom. The responsibility for tomorrow's world lies with the children of today. Cristina Kessler's book reminds us that it is a responsibility we must take seriously if our natural world is to survive.

MSWATI III, INGWENYAMA

His Majesty, King Mswati III, Ingwenyama of the Kingdom of Swaziland

Introduction

The golden light of an African winter morning mingles with the dust stirred up by a happy, chattering crowd. Excitement crackles in the chilly morning air. Suddenly, the movement and voices stop, and silence slips over the crowd. The king has arrived.

King Mswati III, dressed in his finest cloth and red loerie feather, smiles upon the crowd that has gathered to celebrate a very special day in the kingdom of Swaziland.

With a smile as bright as the morning sun, King Mswati III looks at the people gathered. He radiates the exact same qualities as his symbol, the lion. Dignity, strength, and pride flow toward the crowd, which waits expectantly for His Majesty's words.

"Three centuries ago, our ancestors reached the end of a journey. Like their forefathers before them, they had been on a journey to find a land they could call their own, a land that would provide them with all they needed to feed and water their families and their cattle, and with sufficient natural resources to sustain their people for generations to come.

"They found their land here in this lush and fertile area of southern Africa. With plentiful water, good grazing, wide-ranging forests, and rich soil, they had truly discovered a paradise on earth. And they shared the paradise with an abundance of wildlife, whose numbers

Ted "Machobane" Reilly tells King Mswati III a story during the celebration of the lion's return to Swaziland.

Two male impala face off during mating season.

The white rhino is also called the square-lipped rhino. The flat mouth is adapted for grazing. The rhino faces extinction because its horn is coveted by poachers.

Warthogs were among the first animals Reilly brought back to Swaziland.

must have promised never-ending supplies of meat and hunting.

"Well into this century, Swaziland was famous for the size and variety of its wildlife herds and for the large numbers of predators that competed with man in the hunt.

"Could our forefathers have believed, as they marveled at the numbers of game roaming the valleys and forests, that there would come a day when most species of wildlife could no longer call Swaziland home? And yet, independence in 1968 found us celebrating our freedom without the presence in the kingdom of the twin symbols of our nation—the mighty elephant and the majestic lion.

"By the year of my coronation, in 1986, the arrival of the elephant in the kingdom meant that we were missing only one species of mammal to complete the reintroduction program.

"Ladies and gentlemen, we are here today to celebrate the return of the last and most significant beast of them all.

Following my command to Machobane three years ago, the whole of Swaziland trembles once more to the roar of the lion."

Looking to his left, the king bows his head to Machobane in recognition of the thirty years this man has worked for just this moment.

Ted "Machobane" Reilly is a soft-spoken, almost shy man. You wouldn't imagine him wrestling crocodiles, or attaching a harness to a hippopotamus, or chasing wildebeest while riding in a jeep at high speed. He doesn't seem like someone who has shot at animal poachers or advised two kings on matters of conservation. But he has done all these things.

As a child, Ted Reilly never dreamed his family's farm would become the example for the country's future game parks and reserves. He could not have imagined that he would lead the fight to preserve Swaziland's wildlife. Little did Ted Reilly know that one day he would be called *Liso Lenkhosi Etinyamataneni*—"the Eye of the King on Wild Animals."

Red-billed hornbills are very common in the lowveld.

11

In the Beginning

If someone set out to create an ideal refuge for endangered animals, it might look a lot like Swaziland. This small southern African country has all the ingredients needed to support many types of wild animals.

On the western border is highveld—grassy plains rich with forest. From the highveld the land drops to an area of fertile soil and lush vegetation called the "Valley of Heaven." From there, the land continues to drop into the lowveld, covered with thorn trees and savanna grasses. Three main rivers, the Usutu, Ingwavuma, and the Imbuluzi, cross the lowveld plains. They flow through gorges cut into the Lubombo Mountains on their journey to the sea.

The climate of the country supports varied plant and animal life. The winters, from June to August, are warm during the day and cool at night. Summers from November to January get very hot in the grassy lowveld areas.

Swaziland's capital city, Mbabane, sits in the hills to the north of the Valley of Heaven. Much of the surrounding area is

Above, *a lone blesbok grazes on the new grasses during the rainy season in Mlilwane. Opposite, a view of Mlilwane from Poacher's Lookout during the dry season.*

Nguni cattle, which arrived with the Nguni people, were the first domesticated animals in Swaziland. These cattle have been brought back from the edge of extinction.

now farmland. In their daily life and culture, the Swazi people are closely connected to the land and its wildlife.

King Mswati III rules with total authority. The king and his council gather regularly to discuss and settle affairs of the nation. They make rulings that preserve and protect wildlife. They are continuing the work of Mswati III's father, King Sobhuza II, who began the modern conservation movement. Their efforts reflect a long tradition of respect for nature that began with the country's first people.

Swaziland's earliest residents were the San. These short, sturdy people lived in total harmony with their surroundings. For thousands of years they wandered across southern Africa. Living in small groups, the San collected wild plants and fruits, pods and berries. They hunted to feed themselves or to appease their ancestors with ceremonial offerings. The land remained unchanged as both people and wild animals thrived.

In the fifteenth century the Nguni people from the north moved into the region. The ancestors of the modern Swazi people brought with them domesticated cattle and a system of farming. They changed the land, but a balance with nature still existed. Nguni cattle grazed on the plains side by side with wild herds of wildebeest, zebras, impala, warthogs, and rhinoceroses.

The first European settlers arrived in Swaziland in the 1850s. Their records describe vast herds covering the land.

The blue wildebeest have nearly been wiped out twice in Swaziland, but now there are well-established herds once again.

Giraffe, impala, kudu, and rhinoceros roamed as far as the eye could see. The Europeans' arrival signaled dramatic changes for Swaziland's wildlife.

The settlers hunted game in large numbers for sport. But a far greater problem was a disease that spread from the north in 1886. Contaminated cattle carried rinderpest disease from Europe to North Africa. This deadly virus passed from domestic cattle to wild animals that

A herd of impala gathers at the large wetland area in Mlilwane. Only male impala have horns.

shared their grazing land.

The Cattle Plague swept south across Africa killing domestic and wild herd animals in its path. By 1896 it had reached Swaziland and killed almost the entire populations of impala, roan antelope, hartebeest, and wildebeest.

The disappearing herds left Swaziland's fertile highlands and the lowveld empty. European settlers quickly moved onto the land. They raised sheep and cattle where wildebeest had wandered and antelope once grazed. They cleared land and planted cotton and corn. Their lives were going well until 1930, when something incredible occurred.

One day countless thousands of wildebeest arrived from the north. The herds were so large they filled the horizon from one sunrise to the next. It had taken thirty years, but the wildebeest herds had finally recovered from the Cattle Plague. When the herds grew large enough to deplete their grazing areas, they migrated south and west in search of food as their ancestors had done before.

The wildebeest plowed through fences and trampled fields. They ate all the grass and crops that they could find, leaving cattle starving and settlers furious.

Angry farmers and ranchers declared war on the so-called "Wildebeest Scourge." They hunted from jeeps and trucks with mounted machine guns. They poisoned water holes and troughs, wiping out all types of game.

Around the same time, settlers began large-scale killing of plains game for another reason. When pig farming was introduced in Swaziland, wild game became a cheap, easy source of food. Farmers began killing roan antelope, impala, waterbuck, and zebra by the thousands to make feed for their pigs.

In the past one hundred years many animals vanished from the Swazi landscape. Giraffe disappeared during the Cattle Plague. Elephants soon followed. The fastest antelope, the tsessebe, was lost in the 1930s. The last resident lion was shot in 1954. The last roan antelope died in a poacher's snare in 1961.

The land was changing rapidly, too. People turned wild habitats into farms and plantations. Survival for the few animals that remained seemed impossible. If any wildlife were to exist in Swaziland, then sanctuaries had to be created. It was at this moment that Ted Reilly stepped forward and faced the challenge.

The tsessebe, with its long face and sloping back, is often considered the ugliest animal in Africa. Actually, it is the fastest antelope and lives in small family groups.

Ted Reilly Starts at Mlilwane

Ted Reilly was born in Swaziland in 1938 on the family farm, called Mlilwane. As a child, he spent his days with the young herders who worked there. He passed the time watching animals and learning the secrets of the bush from his friends.

When he was five years old, Ted's mother found him in the garden. He was using a small hose to bore holes into a bank of earth. "I'm making homes for kingfisher birds," he explained. The kingfishers soon discovered the nests. Ted's life as a caretaker of wild animals had begun.

When he was eighteen Reilly started his official conservation training in Natal, South Africa. He spent two years at Sabi Sand Game Reserve. He later worked on several conservation projects in the neighboring countries of Northern Rhodesia (Zambia) and Rhodesia (Zimbabwe). Then in 1960 it seemed as if his career would be cut short. Reilly's mother called him home. His father had died years before while Ted was at school, but in 1960 his mother needed Ted's help to run the farm.

The final leg of his trip home was a two-hundred-kilometer trek across the Swazi countryside. When he was twelve years old, Ted had traveled the same roads with his father. For a young boy who loved animals, it had been a magnificent journey. "I was never out of sight of game," he recalls. "There were wild animals all over Swaziland."

Reilly retraced his steps in 1960. What he saw stunned him. Conditions in Swaziland had changed drastically. "In ten years the game had been decimated," Ted says. "I didn't see one wild animal along the way. I was shocked!"

By the time he reached home, Reilly knew his future was not in farming. He wanted to save wildlife in his homeland. Although he had the skills, he had no money and no place to begin. Reilly did the only thing he could. He dedicated his family's farm to the cause.

Mlilwane lies in the Valley of Heaven. It is surrounded by Swaziland's most historic mountains: Execution Rock, Sheba's Breasts, and the Mdzimba Range. The Mhlambanyatsi River runs through the land, now blocked to form the

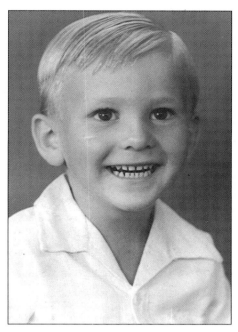

Ted Reilly, 1943

A crocodile basks in the sun.

river running through Mlilwane. These created wetland areas where hot or thirsty animals could gather. After introducing water plants into the two new lakes, the next challenge began.

Reilly went on safari with his team of ten park rangers-in-training. They needed to find animals to fill the wetlands. They traveled to nearby public land and caught frogs, fish, water scorpions, and insects. Ted quickly discovered that each success presented new and riskier challenges.

"After a thriving population of barble catfish was established in the small lakes, it was time to look for the next creature up the food chain—crocodiles," recalls Ted. The rangers captured their first crocodile on the bank of the Nkomati River, just north of Mlilwane. With the angry nine-foot reptile in the back of a pickup truck, they raced to the sanctuary. The crocodile was deposited in one of the lakes, and the work continued.

Reilly searched up and down the food chain, finding animals wherever he could. Several turtles were brought from local rivers. In 1967 the first hippopotamus came from South Africa. By this time birds had returned to the area, and the wetlands were firmly established.

Reilly was changing the rest of the farm, too. He hoped to reintroduce herds of grazing animals at Mlilwane. He planted tall grasses on the fertile land. When grass covered the plains, he approached King Sobhuza II and asked for his help.

wetlands in the sanctuary. Mlilwane had been in the Reilly family since 1906, when Ted's father arrived from South Africa where he had fought with British troops in the Boer War. For nearly fifty-five years this successful farm produced beef, fruit, rice, timber, and corn. However, farming and other activities had changed the land. To make Mlilwane a suitable sanctuary, Reilly first had to restore the wildlife habitat.

Ted began with a major tree-planting project. He collected seeds from native trees. He grew seedlings and planted them on 460 hectares of farmland.

Next Reilly built two dams on the

The last surviving herds of plains game in the country were living at Hlane. King Sobhuza II had purchased this isolated farmland in 1945 from Swaziland's first conservationist, David Forbes. In spite of the king's wish to protect the animals living there, poachers had killed most of the surviving game.

Reilly showed King Sobhuza II his work at Mlilwane. The king saw hectares of grassland with fencing to keep the animals inside and the poachers outside. The tall grasses covering the plains reminded him of the way his country looked when he was young. He gave Reilly permission to go to Hlane and capture what game he could to transfer to Mlilwane.

Reilly set to work immediately. He and his rangers jumped into an old jeep called Jezebel and drove two hours to Hlane. They raced to beat the poachers to the remaining animals. Jezebel crashed through the bush in high-speed pursuit of game. Over several months they captured wildebeest, zebra, impala, kudu, and waterbuck. They also caught many smaller animals, like genet cats and monitor lizards.

Despite the fencing and patrols by rangers, poachers followed the game to Mlilwane. King Sobhuza II decided to stop them. He called together the chiefs of the region. He commanded them to stop the poaching and let the animals live in peace. Mlilwane was close to the palace, and the king's influence was great. The poaching stopped at once.

Ted knew his wetlands were established when birds began to move into the area. This blue crane and its mate live in Mlilwane.

Three new giraffes arrive in Hlane Royal National Park. They traveled from South Africa in a truck designed for transporting this type of animal.

Still, in other parts of Swaziland problems remained. In 1967 King Sobhuza II sent his royal hunters to Hlane. With the king's blessing and permission, they would kill a small number of animals to be used in a traditional Swazi ceremony. The king was very upset when his hunters returned after several days with only one impala. It was the only animal they had seen.

Now, the king summoned Ted to Masundvwini, his royal residence, for Ted's advice. Reilly explained that the game in Hlane was under constant threat from poachers and from a growing population moving into the area. Hlane and the surrounding region had always been sparsely populated due to a harsh climate, rampant malaria, and little rain. But as the population of the country grew, people moved into areas previously unsettled. Hlane, which means "wilderness," was being surrounded by a permanent population for the first time.

The king realized that if the game of Hlane was to be saved, something needed to be done immediately. Thinking of the success of Mlilwane, the king commanded Reilly to turn Hlane into the country's first national park. On that day Ted received his new title—*Liso Lenkhosi Etinyamataneni*. Reilly and his rangers rose to the challenge of establishing Hlane.

It was expensive, but fifteen thousand hectares of a total of thirty thousand hectares were fenced. Ranger patrols were established, and poachers were actively

pursued. As the poaching slowed, Ted began to restock Hlane with offspring of the game he had taken from there to Mlilwane in its early days. Within a few years there were more than eleven thousand head of mixed game in Hlane.

In 1975 Ted and his wife, Liz, focused on saving the remaining Nguni cattle, which had lived in Swaziland for more than twelve hundred years. They bought four hundred hectares of land in another remote, harsh region of the country and named the place Mkhaya for the species of thorn tree that covers the land. Though unattractive to settlers, Mkhaya was a perfect habitat for the Nguni. The area was fenced, and conservation practices were put into action.

Small game herds began to grow again. Reilly then decided to go one step farther. Historically the Ngunis had lived and grazed with wild game, so why couldn't they again? He decided to make multiple use of the land, bringing browsers and grazers from Hlane and Mlilwane. The grazers, like white rhino and zebra, would share the grasses and ground cover with the Ngunis. The browsers, like black rhino and giraffe, would eat shrubs and trees.

With the fencing in place and ranger patrols protecting the game, the Mkhaya Nguni Ranch became the Mkhaya Nature Reserve in 1981, dedicated to the preservation of lowveld endangered species. It has since been expanded to nearly seven thousand hectares.

War Against Poaching

Today, seventy-three thousand hectares, or four percent of Swaziland, is set aside in national parks and reserves. The entire range of plains game—including wildebeest, waterbuck, impala, kudu, and zebra—mix on the wide grasslands. Their numbers have all grown to solid herd sizes that guarantee continued survival. As the number of animals increases, the focus shifts from growing the populations to protecting them.

Poaching is a critical problem on all of Africa's wildlife preserves. The elephant and rhino populations have suffered the most. The black rhino total has been reduced by ninety-seven percent since 1960, with many experts predicting there will be none left by the year 2000.

All people who hunt in protected areas are poachers, but there are different types of poachers. While some men hunt to fill the family's cook pot, others hunt for profit. Commercial poachers, inspired by the high prices paid for the prized rhino horn or elephant's ivory tusk, tend to be brazen and dangerous. If caught in

Petros "Mabulane" Ngomane, the chief ranger, has worked with Ted since 1960. He is known for his bravery and bush wisdom. His name means "he who walks in hostile places." Opposite, an eerie collection of skulls from rhinos poached in Swaziland.

Snares come in all shapes and sizes. Over the years, the rangers have collected more snares than there are animals in the entire kingdom.

the act, they shoot first, then try to escape. Big money is offered for horns and tusks and rare skins, like that of the leopard.

There is also a lot of money to be made in selling the meat of plains game killed on a large scale. First the poachers set as many as one hundred traps, called snares, on a line near a watering hole or along a game trail. Snares have improved over the past few years. Wire brought in from foreign countries has proven to be of much better quality, making snares more effective and more dangerous.

Some are laid upon the ground, waiting for an animal to step into them. Others are hung from trees, waiting for an animal to walk into them. A noose with a slipknot hangs from a branch or a bush. A lucky animal dies from strangulation in a matter of minutes as it fights against the snare, pulling it tighter and tighter. Sometimes an animal's agony can drag on for weeks or years. If a rhino or elephant gets caught by the leg, the sharp-cutting snare wire can lead to infections and a slow death.

Rangers sweep through the parks searching for snares. Sometimes they pass a snare line and don't see it. When a poacher returns, he may see tracks of the passing ranger and assume an ambush has been set. He flees, leaving the snares in place. "Those snares are just as deadly one month or six months from then," says Ted.

Battling a faceless army of poachers is a small band of forty-two park rangers. Eighteen rangers patrol Hlane. Twelve

protect Mkhaya and twelve defend Mlilwane. The rangers get most of their training through firsthand experience. Some attend classes in South Africa. Since an absent ranger leaves an empty space, courses are kept short.

The poachers are often better equipped than the rangers who battle them. They have high-powered rifles and faster vehicles. Even so, the dedication of the rangers has had a powerful effect.

"A ranger's job isn't a glamorous one," says Ted. "It's a lot of hard work. A lot of hardship. A lot of discomfort. Poachers don't wait for the office to open to come and poach. And they won't go home at five o'clock. They'll come when it's raining or very cold at night. They come at times when everyone wants to be in bed. And so I have the most incredible respect for these rangers."

A typical day begins before the sun rises. Rangers patrol along the fence, searching for places where poachers have attempted to enter during the night. Each man is armed with a rifle and a walkie-talkie in case it is necessary to call for help. They travel in pairs on foot, while

Ted Reilly and his son, Mick, with the majority of park rangers. Mick Reilly joined his father as a ranger in 1994.

Rangers watch for signs of poachers from different places in the parks. Guard towers that stand twenty-five feet tall provide a good vantage point to look for smoke, dust from vehicles, or scavenger birds.

others ride bicycles. They watch the skies for gathering vultures and follow them to the site of a dead animal. And they search the park endlessly for snares and footprints.

A man caught poaching in broad daylight is usually looking for food. He will probably be unarmed and will try to escape on foot without a confrontation. If he is caught, the rangers will take him to park headquarters and then to the nearest police station.

A commercial poacher presents much more danger for the ranger. "During my thirty-seven years as a park ranger," says Ted, "it is an exception to the rule for a commercial poacher to turn himself over without a struggle. Especially at night. You don't know how many there are—two or six or ten men. And you don't know if

you'll live to tell the tale afterward. Arresting poachers at night can be a terrifying experience."

In order to control and punish poaching, Swazi law divides animals into three categories. Specially Protected Game includes endangered animals such as rhinoceros, elephant, and lion. Royal Game contains everything from bush babies to hippopotamus, as well as many types of plains game. The third group, called Common Game, lists animals that are plentiful. Each category is protected by its own set of penalties.

Poachers receive the stiffest sentence for killing game on the Specially Protected Game list. In Swaziland a poacher who kills a rhino, elephant, or lion faces a minimum five years in prison and a fine equal to the value of the animal. If the poacher cannot replace the animal or pay the value of the animal, two years are added to the sentence.

"There is a big difference between the man who kills an impala to feed his family and a man who kills a rhino or elephant or hundreds of impala for sale. But the laws must be enforced across the board," says Ted.

The battle against poaching will never end, but Reilly remains optimistic. "Many of the rangers may not read or write well, but they are clued up and highly intelligent and proficient in the ways of the bush. These are the men who are responsible for the high numbers of game that live in Swaziland today."

The marabou stork is a park cleaner. These birds eat carrion left by other animals or poachers. Rangers will go to areas where storks or vultures are circling to see what dead animals are on the ground.

Somersault and Friends

"There's one family of hippo in Mlilwane and room for only one," says Ted. Somersault, the lone bull hippopotamus, rules the Mlilwane wetlands. He lives there with seven adult females and two female calves.

Somersault arrived from South Africa's Kruger Park in 1967. Reilly planned to import more hippos, but the following year hippos were shown to be susceptible to hoof-and-mouth disease. Officials therefore stopped the movement of the animals, leaving Swaziland with their one lone bull.

When his source from South Africa was cut off, Reilly tried to capture some animals locally. "Pulling a hippo out of a river is a very dangerous job," he explains. "In fact, they are the hardest of all animals to capture and move. Their size has something to do with it, as does their bad tempers."

To capture large wild animals, rangers

Somersault is the lone bull and boss of the Mlilwane wetlands. After twelve long, lonely years, he now has a harem of seven females. He fathered his first two babies in 1992.

31

use darts loaded with tranquilizer. A dart is shot into the muscle of the animal. After a short period of time, the animal falls unconscious. The rangers move in and secure the animal for transport back to the park.

Darting a hippopotamus is risky. The first two hippos Reilly and his rangers darted became frightened. They ran into the water, fell asleep, and drowned. A third hippo was captured on land. Unsedated, she battled a dozen rangers for eighteen hours while being moved to Mlilwane. Ten days later she died. "It was the trauma of the capture that killed her," explains Reilly. "At that point we decided to give up, and hope someone could offer us a captured one to buy."

Somersault lived alone for twelve years. Then in 1979 Reilly met C. G. C. Rawlins, the director of London's Whipsnade Zoo. Ted told him about his search for a mate for Somersault. Rawlins said, "I can give you a hippo. They are born in my zoo every year, and we don't have room to keep them."

At the time, Reilly did not take the conversation seriously. Three months later a cable from London arrived. The zoo had a young heifer. Did Ted want her? "Of course I said yes, then began to tackle the problem of getting a baby hippo from England to Swaziland."

Reilly called South African Airways and explained his problem. Officials there said it would cost 8,000 rand (about $2,500) to fly the hippopotamus to Johannesburg. A

discouraged Reilly thanked them and said he would contact them when he had the funds. He was greatly surprised when airline officials called him back. They would donate the flight to help Swaziland's conservation movement. Ted flew to London to supervise the shipment of the one-year-old hippopotamus.

When Winnie finally arrived, she was coaxed into a large penned area,

Opposite, *Winnie was the first female companion for Somersault.* Above, *two hippos wrestle in the water.*

Lucia was the first hippo to have a baby by Somersault. A baby hippo weighs up to one hundred pounds at birth.

called a boma. "We couldn't release her straight into the water," recalls Ted. "We didn't know how the old bull would handle her—he might just kill her, for one thing." There were also some large crocodiles living in the water. Reilly kept Winnie in a pen until winter. By then she would be bigger, and the crocodiles would be less active in cold water.

For months Somersault and Winnie sniffed one another through the bars of the boma. Winnie shared the pen with two white rhinoceroses.

"When the weather had cooled and Winnie was bigger, we decided it was time to release her," says Ted. "Would Somersault kill her? We didn't know. Instead, he not only accepted her, he became very protective, never leaving her side. We were totally pleased with the results, at first."

A few weeks later, Reilly released the white rhinoceroses. The events that followed shocked everyone. One afternoon, the two animals wandered down to the water for a drink. Somersault came charging out of the water. Within minutes he killed both white rhinoceroses with deadly bites to their throats.

Reilly had never heard of something like this happening. He had established a mating pair of hippos at Mlilwane, but the park had lost two of its rarest animals. It was a terrible loss that reminded Ted how difficult his work would be.

In 1980 Reilly received news of another hippo at the Whipsnade Zoo.

It is rare to see a baby hippo leave the water during the day. Lucia's baby takes a stroll along the water's edge.

This time, it was an adult male. The airlines did not have any cargo planes based in London that were large enough to fit his cage through the loading doors. The animal had to be transferred by truck to the English Channel, then ferried across by boat, and trucked to Paris, France. There it was loaded on a plane with larger doors and flown to Africa.

Ted remembers clearly the madness that resulted when the bull finally arrived: "We decided to release him in Mlilwane because we have two lake areas there. That was a mistake." Somersault became enraged by the newcomer. He chased the bull into the hills, attacking and wounding him. Chaos filled the reserve for a week. "Finally we were able to rescue him and move him to Mkhaya," says Ted.

"He still lives there with two females as the resident reigning bull."

Today there are twenty-three hippos in Swaziland, including Lucia, the first female to give birth to a baby by Somersault. Space is limited, and Ted will have a problem as the population increases. Like the London zoo keeper, he will have to do something with his surplus of hippos.

This problem may provide Swaziland with an opportunity. An adult hippopotamus sells for $5,000. Selling the extra animals may raise money for other park needs. It will also show the success of Swaziland's unique conservation program. In less than thirty years, a country that once imported hippos can send them where they are needed most.

Hippos spend most of the day in the water, or very near it. Somersault leaves the water to graze in the early evening. At night the hippos travel regularly between the two wetlands in search of food.

Return of the Rhino

Ted Reilly has had many amazing encounters with Africa's wild animals. One of Reilly's stories involves the capture of a huge white rhinoceros. He and his men were working with the most basic equipment—a flatbed truck and a dart gun.

It took thirty men three hours to hoist the sleeping one-and-a-half-ton rhino onto the truck's bed. They tied the rhino securely to the truck's deck and climbed aboard. Sitting around its massive, motionless body, they sped toward the nearest boma.

"It was a short distance from the veld to the boma," recalls Ted with a smile, "so we didn't have a crate. We were unprepared for what happened. The rhino awoke from a deep sleep, snapped the ropes, and stood up!"

Suddenly, thirty men and a dazed white rhino were sharing the back of a speeding truck. Six men did not hesitate. They jumped from the speeding vehicle.

The truck zigzagged down the road. Its wobbling at high speed may have helped the situation, for as suddenly as the rhino had risen, it collapsed. After tying it to the

An aerial view from a helicopter of four dehorned rhinos grazing at Hlane Royal National Park. Helicopters are used in counting game over large areas.

Above, *a ten-day-old baby sleeps at its mother's side.* Opposite, *a five-month-old grazes with its mother.*

floor again, twenty men announced they would walk the rest of the way. One ride with a groggy rhino was enough for them. Amazingly, no one, including the men that had jumped from the truck, had been hurt.

The white rhinoceros returned to Swaziland in 1964, seventy years after they had disappeared from the wild. They were a gift to Mlilwane from the Umfolozi Game Reserve in Natal, South Africa. A very successful program at Umfolozi had brought the white rhino population back from the edge of extinction.

Another four white rhino arrived in 1968.

They were gifts to King Sobhuza II from the Natal Parks Board. The rhinos went to Hlane, the best habitat for these great beasts. The area around the reserve was still relatively uninhabited, and the grass was ideal forage for white rhino.

Between 1964 and the early 1970s, Ted acquired more than sixty white rhino from South Africa. The rhinos were considered "troublemakers" in Umfolozi, where there were so many they were moving out into lands worked by local farmers. Ted could have each animal for the cost of capture and transport.

When the animals arrived in Hlane, the rhinos went straight to the bomas, as all animals do. At Umfolozi, these animals had broken out of the park's confines, crossing fence lines as they pleased. When they were suddenly confined within the log walls of a boma, they were not happy.

"Some broke through the log walls separating the pens and either killed each other or combined forces to demolish the outer walls, bashing their way to freedom," recalls Ted. Many of them wandered beyond park boundaries as far away as Mozambique. Even so, by 1980 the herd inside the park grew to 110 animals.

White rhinos were one of many growing populations at Hlane. The rich savanna grass produced grazing herds too large for its capacity. Soon the large wildebeest population ate the land clean. The hungry rhinos quickly took to fence bashing again in search of greener pastures.

The rhinos spread across Swaziland.

Reilly and his rangers tracked them for more than eighty kilometers in all directions. Many of the recovered rhinos had their large behinds riddled with buckshot. Others had snare wounds. Rangers treated the rhinos and released them into the preserve. At the first opportunity they broke out again.

The wandering rhinos were putting themselves at risk. Outside the park they were easy targets for poachers. The 1984 census showed only thirty-six rhinos in and around the park. In four years the population had shrunk by two-thirds.

Something had to be done quickly to save the remaining rhinos. Reilly and his rangers separated the herd into small groups and spread them out in the parks. Smaller, settled populations would be less likely to wander. By dispersing herds more widely in protected areas, he also hoped to minimize the chances for poaching.

Moving adults is a dangerous and often unsuccessful process. They are too big and set in their ways. Instead, Ted moved the weaning group of rhinos who were two years old. The rangers were still working with limited equipment, and the smaller rhinos were easier to handle. The youngsters would also adapt and settle faster in a new home.

Ted knew that moving these young animals had an added benefit. Without the young ones around, mothers mated sooner and reproduction rates picked up. By 1988, the population was back up to seventy-two animals.

In 1987 Reilly shifted his attention to the return of black rhinoceros to Swaziland. This species had disappeared from Swaziland in the late 1800s. Ted unsuccessfully tried to obtain some black rhinos from Rhodesia in the 1960s. With the conservation movement still in its infancy, Swaziland was considered risky for the world's most endangered land mammal.

Reilly kept trying. In 1971 he tried to exchange twelve white rhinos from Swaziland for twelve black rhinos from Rhodesia. When the war for

Although a rhino's horn looks very strong, it is made only of compacted hair.

43

independence in Rhodesia broke out, the plan had to be scrapped. In 1980 the war ended. Once the newly independent country of Zimbabwe was established, Ted renewed trade talks.

By 1987, the poaching in Zimbabwe was wiping out an average of one rhino a day. The World Wide Fund for Nature sponsored a program to save the black rhino in the Zambezi Valley. Officials arranged a rhino swap between Swaziland and Zimbabwe. They offered to cover the costs of relocation, something Reilly never could have afforded.

The swap would only involve twelve animals—six black for six white. A cloak-and-dagger plan emerged to transfer the rhinos. Absolute secrecy was needed to prevent poachers from learning of the plan.

On the night of December 28, 1987, a team of rangers led by Reilly's son, Mick, arrived at Beit Bridge, the border between Zimbabwe and South Africa. After the exchange, the convoy traveled throughout the night across South Africa. It arrived at the Swazi border just after sunrise. Six hours later the first black rhino entered the boma area in Mkhaya.

There are differences between the black and white rhinos. The black is a browser, eating from shrubs and low tree branches. It holds its heavy head farther from the ground than the grazing white rhino. It is also smaller than the white. With its more upright position and smaller size, the black rhino moves faster than its cousin. It is also much more aggressive.

Each new arrival received a Swazi name to fit its personality. The rangers named the large bull Mayaluka, which means "the one who cannot stand still." Khakhayi was "the hardheaded one" and Fecele was "the scorpion." The calmest female was called Lungile, "the all right one." Finally, there were two small aggressive rhinos— Manyovu, "the hornet," and Mbabatane, "the stinging nettle."

Each rhino lived in a separate boma for two months. Reilly wanted to discourage their urge to wander. Although

Black rhinos are browsers and tend to spend the day deep in the bush. They also are extremely shy, which makes them difficult to find. The year 1992 was a bad one for black rhinos in Swaziland. The first baby born in one hundred years died of a snakebite days after birth. Two females died during the drought.

comfortable and well fed, the rhinos were unprepared for life surrounded by an electric fence.

Mayaluka was the first to be released. He walked along, browsing peacefully until he strolled down to the fence and touched it. The fence line, electrified by four thousand volts, jolted him, sending him snorting into the bush. That night Mayaluka returned to the fence. The next morning rangers found a fence gate bent and buckled, but unbroken. Judging from the tracks they followed, the rhino had run for two kilometers after receiving his second shock. That's the last of Mayaluka's known encounters with the fence.

Khakhayi had been released that same day. She stuck her head through the fence and got a shock that sat her on her haunches. She roared with pain and scrambled off into the bush. Khakhayi has not touched the fence again.

After witnessing these encounters, Ted built an intermediate pen strung with electric wire. One by one, the remaining rhinos went into the electrified area. Without fail, one zap sent each rhino running back to its boma, their lessons in electricity completed at a lower voltage.

The rangers then released two more, Lungile and Manyovu. Their visit to the intermediate pen paid off, for they stayed far from the fence. They browsed together for twenty days, then finally wandered their separate ways. The last two to be released were Fecele and Mbabatane. They both stayed far from the fence.

Mkhaya was divided into two areas separated by electric wire. Fecele and Mayaluka were released on opposite sides of the fence, for bulls are extremely territorial. They met for face-offs and territorial displays at the fence. However, neither one touched the electrified wires. The fences allowed Ted to keep two black rhino herds at Mkhaya without the risks of battles.

In 1992 southern Africa suffered its worst drought in seventy-five years. As grazing grass became scarce, Reilly's rangers took down the fence separating the black rhino herds. After three months the first hungry black rhino crossed into the new territory to browse. The two bulls made contact one time. In the battle that followed, Mayaluka lost half of his horn. Both bulls have established new territories within the reserve and now avoid each other.

On March 10, 1992, poachers killed their first rhino in Mkhaya. On his early morning patrol a ranger came across the shocking sight of a dead rhino with its horn missing. The tracks of the poachers were followed until the trail died. Reilly was outraged. Until that date, rhinos had only been shot in Hlane and outside park areas.

Poaching was becoming an increasingly serious problem. A rhinoceros horn is made of a few pounds of compacted hair. It should be of no use to anyone but the animal. However, in parts of the world, people covet rhinoceros horn.

Above, *Ted digs in a hole started by an elephant or buffalo looking for water. Smaller animals drink from these holes after the big ones leave.* Opposite, *a rhino takes a cool break in a mud hole.*

In the Far East it is wrongly believed to have value as a medicine and an aphrodisiac. In Yemen a dagger handle made of rhino horn is a status symbol. Although it is illegal, people pay a high price for a rhinoceros horn. Dealers charge $10,000 for one kilogram of rhino horn. The poacher receives much less. Even so, poachers in Swaziland have become brazen.

In response to the rise in rhino slaughtering, Reilly moved the rhinos closer to the rangers' camp in Hlane and Mkhaya. Still, at night, poachers shot two pregnant white rhinos only four hundred meters from the ranger's camp in Hlane.

In a drastic attempt to stop the poaching, Ted and his rangers captured the remaining thirteen white rhinos at Hlane and removed their horns. Dehorning does not harm a live rhino, but it is extremely controversial. Should people deform an animal to save it? And will this desperate step stop poachers?

Ted believes dehorning works. In at least two cases, rangers have discovered the tracks of poachers following rhinos. It was clear from the tracks that the poachers had caught up with the rhinos and then let them be. "Since it happened twice, it can be assumed that dehorning must have saved the rhinos' lives," says Ted.

The entire security system has been tightened up, and the laws made stronger. Rangers patrol Hlane and Mkhaya twenty-four hours a day, and there have been obvious results. "During one period, we were losing one rhino every two weeks. A combination of continuous patrols and two poachers killed in a shoot-out has made a big difference. We haven't lost a rhino for twenty months now," says Ted with relief.

Swaziland now has forty rhinos in all. The white rhino group of thirty-six has several solid families that can continue to sustain the breed. The four black rhinos may form a nucleus for breeding, but as Ted points out, "We need more animals to get them going and make them really viable and safe from extinction."

The Elephants Arrive

Both praise and criticism have followed Ted Reilly for his work in Swaziland. Few projects created more controversy than his attempt to bring elephants to Swaziland. In 1986 Reilly acquired two young male elephants from Kruger Park in South Africa.

Kruger Park is a wildlife preserve with land and food to support seventy-five hundred elephants. It has the unusual problem of being overpopulated. Too many elephants can destroy a habitat that provides food and shelter for other animals. Powerful elephants uproot trees to reach the green leaves growing near the top. They strip off the bark of others—and these trees die.

To correct the situation, officials have launched a major culling program. Some animals are killed to help ensure the survival of the rest of the herd and surrounding plant and animal life. When culling elephants, rangers remove whole family groups from the herd. This maintains the natural social structure of the remaining population.

Not all elephants in a culled family

group are killed. Weaned elephants that can be handled are often captured. These smaller animals are easier to transport and adapt more readily to a new environment.

When young elephants were brought to Swazi, critics argued that they could not survive on their own. Elephants have a very strong matriarchal society. The cows train the young until the bulls move into bachelor herds and the females

A young elephant strips bark off a tree.

When young elephants first arrive, they spend time in a boma like all new big animals. Above, *a baby stretches its trunk through the bars looking for food outside.* Opposite, *two juveniles share a boma.*

become mothers. Local critics accused Reilly of taking too big a chance by bringing in young elephants without their mothers.

In building his parks Reilly has often made choices out of necessity. "Yes, the elephants would be better off at their mother's side," admits Ted, "but their mothers are dead. So would they be better off in this instance?"

The first two elephants to enter Swaziland were young males. Reilly chose Mkhaya for their home. The elephants arrived from South Africa during a driving rainstorm. The storm had swollen the river at the entrance to Mkhaya, making it impassable. Rangers brought the elephants to Mlilwane instead.

"The ellies remained at Mlilwane for three months because the public enjoyed them so much," explains Ted. Unfortunately Mlilwane does not have the habitat to sustain elephant. Since the elephants were expensive to feed, Reilly finally decided to move them.

Many people wanted the elephants to remain in Mlilwane, but Ted was adamant. "I've lived through many years of critics yapping at my heels," he says. "In determining where to put any species in the parks of Swaziland, my first concern is for the animal, not for the whim of those who want it some other way."

As an experiment, Reilly released the elephants in Mkhaya. Rangers observed them for a full year. "We wanted to make sure that the elephants could survive here.

We decided it was better to test with two rather than a whole herd," says Ted. The elephants settled in Mkhaya quickly with no obvious side effects from being on their own.

At the end of a year, Ted applied for eighteen more elephants from South Africa. Dr. Anton Rupert, president of the Southern Africa World Wildlife Fund, presented a herd of ten to King Mswati III as a birthday gift and gave eight to Mkhaya. Reilly then purchased eight more to round out the herd.

Once again, all the elephants brought in were young ones whose mothers had been culled in South Africa. Two died shortly after arrival from the trauma of being captured and transported. Three others were killed at Mkhaya by the larger juvenile bulls. The rangers immediately separated the elephants into size groups to protect the smaller animals.

In 1993 an international animal welfare group that opposes culling as a conservation practice offered Reilly $60,000 to establish more elephants in Swaziland—provided that the animals were from an adult group. Reilly turned down the offer. "As reluctant as we were to forego such a large sum of money, we couldn't take the chance of introducing adults into our herds," says Ted.

Doing so, he feared, might disrupt the herds. If adults started breaking out, and the young ones followed, chaos could ensue. "This would be putting the neighboring humans at risk, and any

escaping elephants would have to be shot. That was a risk we weren't willing to take.

"We're eight years down the road with established populations from the original young weaned animals taken from culling. They are very stable, settled, and placid, with no signs of social disorder."

Three young elephants enjoy the cooling mud during the drought of 1992.

Mkhulu was one of the first elephants to arrive in Swaziland in one hundred years. He is the reigning bull at Mkhaya.

Swaziland now has thirty-nine very happy not-so-juvenile elephants that are flourishing and are there for all to see and enjoy. Mkhaya has seventeen elephants, and twenty-two live in Hlane. "If we had listened to the naysayers, we would not have any," says Ted.

Poaching has not yet been a problem for the elephants. Ted and his rangers realize that they will face a real threat when the elephants and their tusks are full grown. For now, the biggest problem is snares set by poachers for other animals. These traps can cripple an elephant if not removed right away.

The resident elephants have not started to reproduce yet, but should do so within the next few years. This will be a crucial test for the young elephants and Reilly's program. Will the females know how to raise their young if not taught by their own mothers? Will there be a breakdown in the social process or the skills of a new mother? In any situation where one is trying new things, the outcome cannot be predicted. But since the elephants are functioning well within their present family groups, Ted is hopeful.

The elephants are beginning to show signs of sexual maturity, and Ted hopes to see new calves within the next three years. For now, though, there are thirty-nine elephants in Swaziland, a very respectable number considering that for nearly one hundred years there weren't any.

Epilogue

Ted Reilly drives leisurely through Hlane Royal National Park as we search for lions. The grass is tall yet dry and brown from months with no rain. Glancing in his rearview mirror, he says quietly, "Look behind us."

There, sauntering up the track, is the male. With the stateliness of a king, he walks slowly, muscles flexing and mane flowing around his huge head. He reaches a clearing and sits, so different from the shy animal of 1994.

The females approach from behind him, followed by a scraggly line of seven nine-month-old cubs. The cubs greet their father, then collapse around him like stuffed toys.

With awe Ted says, "King Mswati III is very proud of this pride. With these cubs we now know that the lion is back to stay in Swaziland."

Many changes have occurred since this book was written in 1994. Between 1995 and 1996, ten cheetahs were reintroduced from Namibia. We were lucky, for we saw three juveniles during our visit. Silently we watched as they played and groomed themselves.

Left, *a female kudu glances up from grazing. Kudus are easily identified by the stripes across their backs and their large ears.* Above, *a young female nyala. Nyalas were among the first antelopes reintroduced to the kingdom.*

A leopard keeps watch from a lofty spot.

The year 1996 also saw the arrival of five leopards, also from Namibia. Three have been released into the park, but two new arrivals are still in the boma. When we were in the park, the male leopard had just finished an impala lunch. He didn't even acknowledge our presence, but his mate did. With a quick look over her shoulder, she gracefully climbed a tree, not stopping until she was at the top.

The cats are not the only news in Swaziland. In 1995 the president of Taiwan presented King Mswati III with six black rhinos. These rare creatures have dispersed into the park at Mkhaya. Ted will not release their exact numbers in order to protect the rhinos, saying only, "Some have had babies, creating a viably sustainable population."

Another guarded secret is the number of white rhinos. All the mature females have produced babies in the past eighteen months. Of those babies, 77 percent are males, which is unfortunate, for it would be better for the population to have that many more females. Poaching is way down. No rhinos have been shot since 1993, and all other herd numbers are up.

Winnie the hippo has given birth to her first baby, and the elephant population has increased with an untold number of new juveniles from South Africa. Ted Reilly is a happy man. "It's like a realization of a great dream," he says.

Succeeding in this dream has not been easy. Droughts, poachers, financial problems, and plenty of critics have blocked the way. But through it all, Ted kept his eye on the ultimate goal—the return of Swaziland's wildlife and, with it, a precious part of his country's heritage.

Despite great odds, Swaziland is again home to animals that lived there long before man's arrival. Thanks to King Sobhuza II, King Mswati III, Ted Reilly, his wife, Liz, and a dedicated staff of rangers, the kingdom of Swaziland is a true success story in the world of conservation—a modern-day Noah's ark.

*Traditional dancers perform for
King Mswati III the day the lions arrive.*

Pronunciation Guide to SiSwati

SiSwati is the national language of Swaziland. It is spoken by all Swazis as well as more than five hundred thousand people in South Africa.

It is a "click" language of the Nguni people, part of the Bantu language group. Their early intermarriage with the San led to the introduction within the language of some San "clicks," which are beautiful to hear.

SiSwati is closely related to Xhosa and Zulu, two other Bantu languages. Speakers of these languages can easily understand siSwati, and vice versa.—C. K.

Boma—BO-MA
Fecele—FÉ-CÉ-LÉ
Hlane—KLAN-NÉ
Imbuluzi—EE-MB-LOO-ZEE
Ingwavuma—EEN-GWA-VU-MA
Ingwenyama—EEN-GWÉ-NYA-MA
Khakhayi—KHA-KHA-YEE
Liso Lenkhosi Etinyamataneni—LEE-SO
    LÉN-KHO-SEE É-TI-NYA-MA-TA-NÉ-NEE
Lubombo—LOO-BO-MBO
    [ɓ]
Lungile—LOO-NGI-LÉ
Mabulane—MA-BU-LA-NÉ
    [ɓ]
Machobane—MA-CHO-BA-NÉ
    [ɓ]
Manyovu—MA-NYO-VOO
Masundvwini—MA-SU-N-DVWEE-NEE
Mayaluka—MA-YA-LOO-KA

Mbabane—MM-BA-BA-NÉ
    [ɓ]
Mbabatane—MM-BA-BA-TA-NÉ
    [ɓ]
Mdzimba—MM-DZEE-MM-BA
Mhlambanyatsi—MM-KLA-MM-BA-NYA-TSEE
Mkhaya—MM-KAA-YA
Mkhulu—MM-KHU-LOO
Mlilwane—MM-LIL-WHA-NÉ
Mswati—MM-SWA-TEE
Ngomane—NGO-MA-NÉ
Nguni—N-GU-NEE
Nkomati—NN-KO-MA-TEE
Sobhuza—SO-BOO-ZA
Umfolozi—OO-MM-FO-LO-ZEE
Usutu—LOO-SU-TU
Zambezi—ZA-MBE-ZEE

Note the pronunciation of the following syllables:
A—as in **a**rch
É—as in **e**gg
EE—as in **ea**se
KH—as in **c**old
KL—as in (similar to the English) **cl**ass; **cl**ean
NG—as in si**ng**
NY—as in ca**ny**on
O—as in **o**ar; sh**o**re
OO—as in **oo**ze; c**oo**l
some **B**'s [ɓ] have no equivalent in English

(The publisher wishes to thank Professor Lwandle C. L. Kunene, associate professor of African languages at the University of Swaziland, for preparing this guide.)

62

INDEX

Numbers in ***boldface*** refer to illustrations or illustration captions on the pages noted.

Acknowledgments

So often, only African disasters get attention. This is a book celebrating an African success story.

Many people made this book possible. I would like to offer a special thank-you to His Majesty, King Mswati III, for writing the foreword that appears in this book and for his dedication to conservation.

Thanks to Swaziland's park rangers Petros Ngomane, Sam Mashaba, Dennis Zishwili, John Magagula, Edison Matsebula, and all the others for their patience and help. Thanks to Liz Reilly, Mick Reilly, and Nellie Shabangu.

I also would like to thank my husband, Joe, and good friend Valerie Dickson-Horton for their support and assistance. Thanks, too, to my editor, Andy Gutelle.

And a very special thanks to Ted Reilly, who took time from his always busy schedule to answer an endless list of questions. There would be no book without his cooperation.

Thank you, one and all—and long live the animals of Swaziland.—C. K.

Baby Cape buffalo

Copyright © 1995, 1997 by Cristina Kessler
All rights reserved

Published by Caroline House
Boyds Mills Press, Inc.
A Highlights Company
815 Church Street
Honesdale, Pennsylvania 18431
Printed in Singapore

Publisher Cataloging-in-Publication Data
Kessler, Cristina.
    All the king's animals : the return of endangered wildlife to Swaziland / written and photographed by
Cristina Kessler.—1st ed.
[64]p. : col. ill. ;   cm.
Includes index and pronunciation guide.
Foreword by Mswati III, king of Swaziland.
Summary : Factual account of how Swaziland, with the effort of native conservationist Ted Reilly and the approval of the
king, restored its native wildlife, which was once lost due to poaching and disease.
ISBN 1-56397-364-2
1. Endangered species—Juvenile literature. 2. Swaziland—Juvenile literature. 3. Wildlife reintroduction—Swaziland—
Juvenile literature. [1. Endangered species. 2. Swaziland. 3. Wildlife reintroduction—Swaziland.] I. Title.
591.529—dc20   1995   CIP
Library of Congress Catalog Card Number 94-79621

First edition, 1995
Book designed by Jeffrey E. George
Maps created by Tom Powers
The text of this book is set in 12-point Stone Serif.

10 9 8 7 6 5 4 3 2